This book belongs to:

Niles's Surprise Visit

By Ginger Smith
Illustrated by DG

Published by Ginger L. Smith
Philadelphia, Pennsylvania

Printed in the United States of America
ISBN: 978-0-578-90004-9

Editing, Illustrations, Book Cover Design, Layout, & Formatting by DG Self-Publishing
www.dgselfpublishing.com

Dedication

Thank you to my children, family, and friends, who have continued to be major sources of inspiration and support throughout my initial process as a first-time author and now with Niles's Surprise Visit, my second book. Thank you for being my biggest cheerleaders, ushering me along and helping reaffirm that I have something of value that both inspires and resonates with all my readers.

Acknowledgments

Thank you to all the educators and youth-based programs who gave me the opportunity to share my story with students through both in-person and online platforms and helped build my confidence in delivering my "baby" to the world.

Thank you, Tiffany Bacon, Communications Extraordinaire, for giving me the opportunity to promote my first release, Niles's Surprise Discoveries, through an online author interview and spotlight on WRUD Radio—Philadelphia shortly after my launch.

Thank you, Christopher Weaver, my PR guru, for being my anchor throughout my process as I wrote both of my books. Your assistance has been invaluable in helping to coach, guide, and support me in brainstorms and in expanding and perfecting my vision for greatness.

Thank you, Lance Wright, my friend, colleague, and fatherhood advocate, who promotes the importance, inclusion, and celebration of fathers everywhere.

Thank you, Donald and Shamirrah Hill, for helping me to realize and achieve my lifelong dream! I am forever indebted to you for the care, knowledge, compassion, and coaching that empowered me and gave me the essential tools to produce two great children's books that I can be extremely proud of and that are the pillars of my legacy foundation.

One warm fall afternoon, Niles wished summer could last just a little longer. Summer was his favorite season. Throughout the summer, Niles had experienced a few surprises and milestones.

For starters, he received a special race car flip watch for his birthday, which helped him keep perfect time. He finally learned how to ride his bike without training wheels, and he and Mama had ridden on a bike trail they had just discovered. Niles had also grown a whole inch and a half taller. He was becoming bigger and stronger every day.

However, his most exciting milestone was getting a personal tour of the animal rescue on Canary Street. This happened after he had found a baby squirrel and learned that his friend Mr. Williams was a retired veterinarian! (That's an animal doctor.)

All of these special milestones were super exciting, but one thing was missing. Niles wished he could share them all with his daddy. Daddy was a pilot in the military and was away on a special mission.

He was part of a unit responsible for giving aid to countries in need. He flew planes that delivered essential supplies such as food, toiletries, medicines, and clothing. Niles's daddy had special advanced pilot training, and helping people was the best part of his job.

Niles was super proud of Daddy. Mama helped Niles write letters to Daddy, and they got to see each other on Zoom once or twice a month. Niles would talk a mile a minute when chatting with Daddy. He wanted to be sure not to leave out any exciting details of his latest adventures.

Daddy was extremely proud of his son. He loved and missed his boy so much. He raved about Niles being super brave and strong in his absence.

One day while sorting the laundry, Mama noticed just how much her strong boy Niles had outgrown his clothes. They all looked so very small. The time had clearly come to donate them to the local shelter down on Spring Garden Drive.

After several weeks of organizing Niles's clothes, Niles and Mama were finally ready to deliver them to the shelter. Niles hoped that some lucky little boy would appreciate his dinosaur sweatshirt. It was his absolute favorite!

As he put the last of the shirts into the boxes, he sang his colors in Spanish: "Rojo, blanco, amarillo, and azul. I can say my colors in Spanish—how cool!"

One by one, Niles placed each shirt and pair of pants into the boxes. He added an extra box filled with some of his old toys and books, as well. Niles loved the idea of sharing his things with another little boy. He hoped they would make that other boy extra happy.

Mama and Niles headed outside to the car to begin loading up the boxes. Niles had not realized just how heavy they were. He was trying his best to use all his strength. When he got within a few steps of the car, Niles heard a strong, familiar voice from behind him.

"Looks like you've got a heavy load there. Let me give you a hand."
Niles knew that warm, chocolatey voice.

His heart began to race really, really fast, and his palms felt sweaty.

Niles closed his eyes, silently counted to three, and quickly spun around. When he opened his eyes, there was Daddy standing on the sidewalk in full uniform!

"Daddy, Daddy, it's you . . . you came home!" Niles shouted and jumped straight into his arms. Daddy and Niles hugged for what seemed like an eternity. It had been almost two full years since they had last seen each other in person.

One single tear trickled down Niles's cheek, but it wasn't because he was sad. It was because he was happy.

"Wow, look at my fine boy!" Daddy beamed with pride. "You have certainly grown, Niles. It is one thing to look at your pictures, but seeing your growth in person is truly amazing! It's so good to be home."

"Daddy, you really surprised me!" Niles replied.

"Yes, Mama and I decided to keep my visit home top secret. I was not due home for several more months, but I was able to make an early return just to see you!"

At that moment, Niles's heart felt full with love. He was so lucky to have a daddy whose love for him was so strong that Niles could feel it from even thousands of miles away. And it felt even better in person, just like the day that Niles was born.

Just then, Niles heard a faint little bark. As he peered down from Daddy's strong shoulders and arms, he noticed a tiny black puppy wagging his tail near Daddy's boots. "Daddy, who is that?!" Niles exclaimed.

"It's a puppy. Your puppy, to be exact," Daddy chuckled. "I was so proud to hear about your recent trip to the animal rescue and your wanting to become a veterinarian. Mama and I decided that you were ready for your first pet."

Niles let go of his firm grip on Daddy and jumped down onto the sidewalk for a closer look at his new pet friend. "What's his name?" Niles asked. "Well, that's for you to decide, son. What would you like to call him?"

Niles thought for a few moments. Then he excitedly blurted out, "Panther . . . Black Panther!"

"I think that's a fine name," said Daddy. "I knew you would pick the perfect name for your new pet."

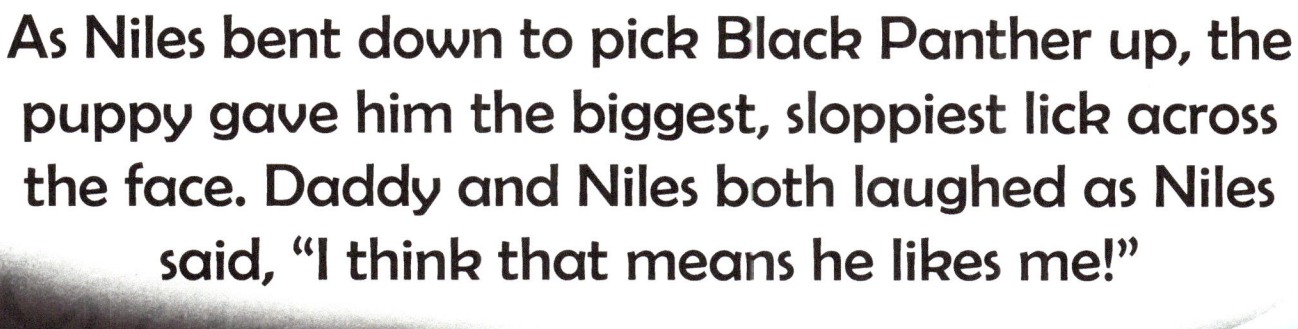

As Niles bent down to pick Black Panther up, the puppy gave him the biggest, sloppiest lick across the face. Daddy and Niles both laughed as Niles said, "I think that means he likes me!"

Niles was so excited about Daddy being home and about his new puppy that he started talking really, really fast. "Oh Daddy, oh Daddy, oh Daddy, can we take Black Panther along for the ride to the shelter?"

"That sounds like a perfect plan, son," Daddy replied. "After we drop the boxes off at the shelter, you, Black Panther, and I can head over to the park. Then we can begin teaching him some fun new tricks!"

Niles scooped up Black Panther, and they piled into the back seat. As they did, Niles rapped, "I'm so happy that my Daddy is home . . . he brought me a new puppy, and I'll never be alone."

Share Your Feedback!

Did you enjoy this book? Please post a review on Amazon to let others know about your experience. Your review will help with getting this book into the hands of more children, and we would love to hear your feedback!